The Moose's Bedtime Routine

Written & Illustrated By: Adam DeRose

To my kids...Now go to bed already!!!

Each night after dinner, the Moose gets ready for bed.

To wind down, he will play ball,

Or with his cars.

If he is stinky, which is most nights, he will take a shower.

But he prefers to take a bath because he can play with his toys.

Once he is squeaky clean, he will brush his teeth.

To get ready for bed, the Moose will avoid a late night snack, like candy, because it will make him hyper.

He says "no" to TV because it will keep him awake.

The Moose will pass on a hot cup of coffee, even if it is decaf.

He will even refuse water or juice because he doesn't want to be up all night going to the bathroom.

Speaking about the bathroom, the Moose will make one last pitstop before bed. And yes, he will wash his little hooves after his business in the bathroom.

Once he is ready for bed, the Moose will go up to his room, and grab a few books to read.

Before getting settled in for the night, the Moose will turn on his night light. He thinks it will help keep the Ghost, Boogie Man, and Shark away.

Then the Moose will close his eyes and drift off to sleep.

He might have a pleasant dream about dancing sugar plums,

Or flying,

Or even driving a monster truck.

He could even have visions about being a pirate.

Being chased,

Or falling.

By the next morning, the Moose was fully recharged, and ready to seize the day!

ABOUT THE AUTHOR

Adam DeRose was born in Buffalo, New York and raised in South Central Grand Island, New York. After graduating from St. Joseph's Collegiate Institute, he attended Daemen College on a Cross Country Scholarship. While running cross country, he met his future wife Shannon. In 2007, Adam received a BS in Art from Daemen College. He continued his education and in 2011, he earned An Associate's Degree in Automotive Technology from Monroe Community College. He currently lives in Rochester, New York with his wife and two kids.

37022036R00029

Made in the USA
Middletown, DE
23 February 2019